ABC in Washington, DC

All 'Bout Cities

Murray Hill Books LLC
www.murrayhillbooks.com

Aa

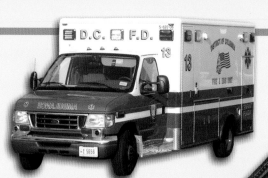

ambulance

automatic teller machine
(ATM)

apartment
building

Arlington Memorial and Roosevelt Bridges

Bb

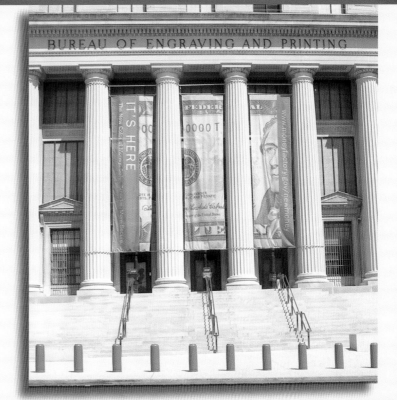

Bureau of Engraving and Printing

bus stop

bus

bench

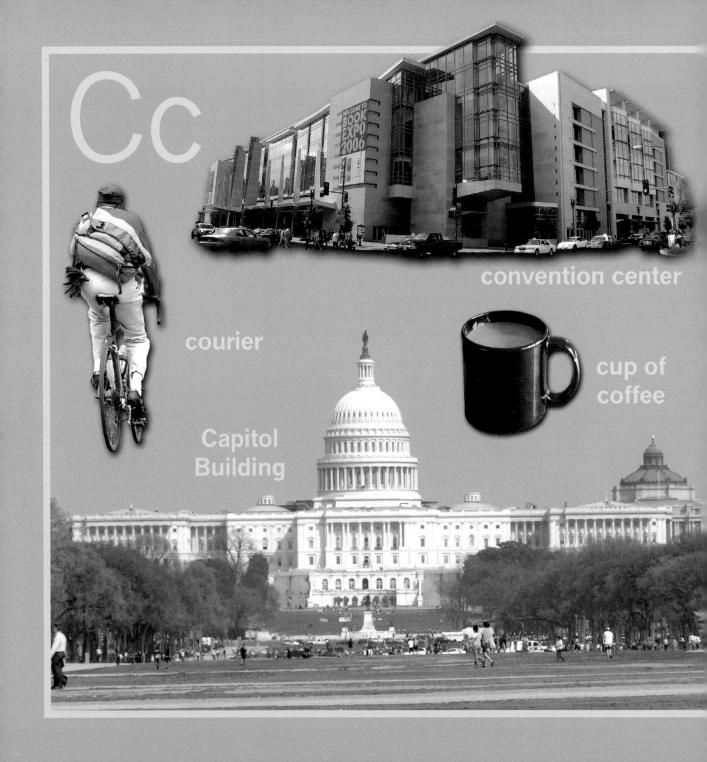

Cc

courier

convention center

cup of
coffee

Capitol
Building

C&O Canal
ational Historic Park

cherry blossoms

construction
crane

cathedral

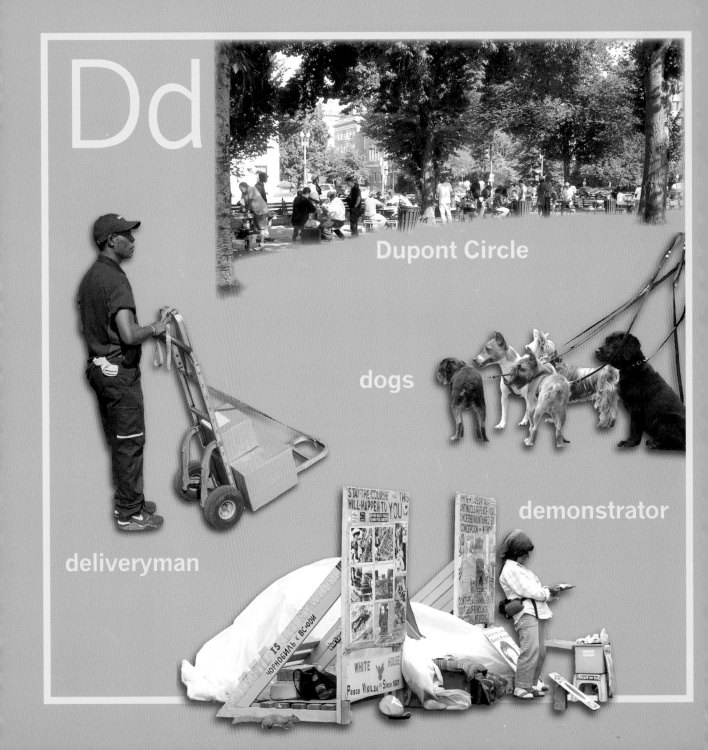

Dd

Dupont Circle

dogs

demonstrator

deliveryman

Ee

elevator

escalators

Eastern Market

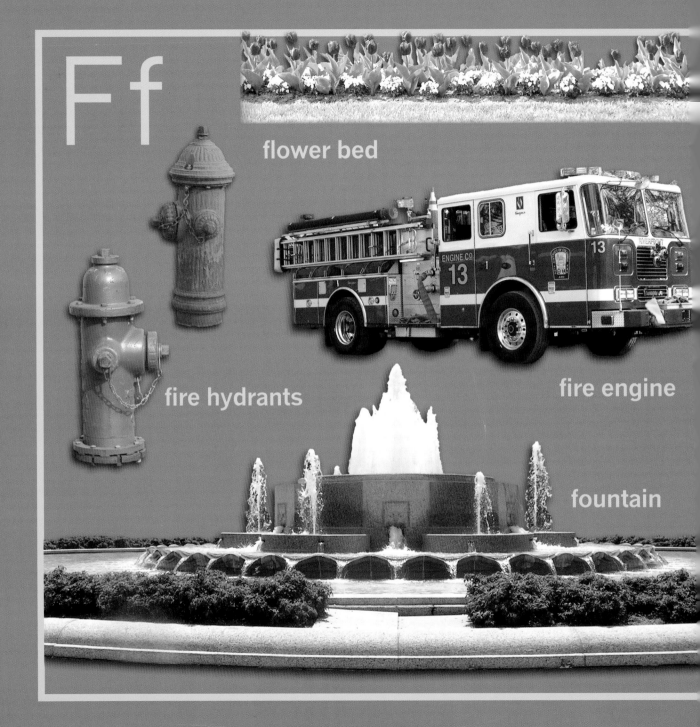

F f

flower bed

fire hydrants

fire engine

fountain

farecard

Friendship Arch

firefighters

flag

Gg

graffiti

Georgetown

Hh

Hirshorn Museum

houses

hot dog

Howard University

Ii

ice cream
sandwich

ice cream
vendor

ICE CREAM

No Ice Cream or Soda allowed
in the Monuments or Memorials

ICE CREAM

No Ice Cream or Soda allowed
in the Monuments or Memorials

Independence Avenue

Jj

joggers

Jefferson
Memorial

Kk

Kutz Bridge

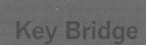

Key Bridge

Kennedy Center

Ll

license plate

limousine

lamppost

Lincoln Memorial

Mm

mail boxes

mail carrier

mail truck

metro
station
marker

Dupont Circle Station

money

manhole cover

map

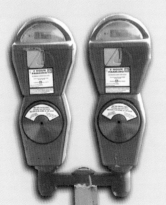

meters

Nn

newspaper
vending machines

news crew

Oo

**Old
Executive
Office
Building**

Pp

pigeons

patrol car

Pennsylvania Avenue

pay pho...

pizza on a paper plate

police officer

pandas

planter

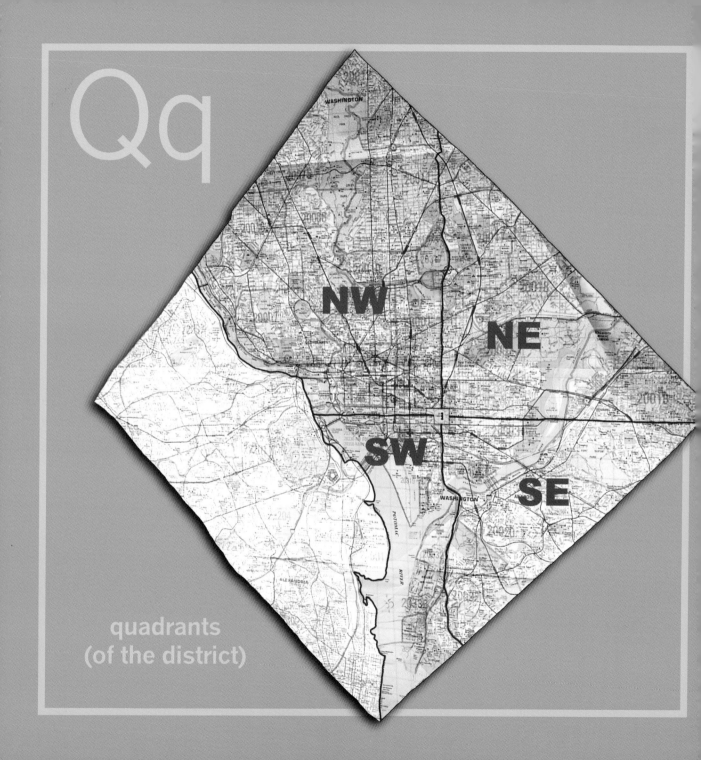

Qq

NW

NE

SW

SE

quadrants
(of the district)

Rr

Reflecting Pool

Rock Creek Parkway

Beyond this Point...

NO SMOKING	NO FOOD OR DRINK	NO WADING
NO BICYCLES	NO SKATEBOARDING	NO RUNNING

rules and restrictions

Ss

squirrel

snack
seller

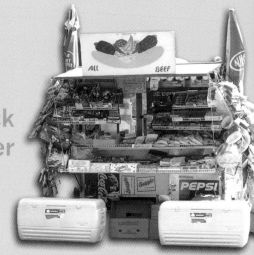

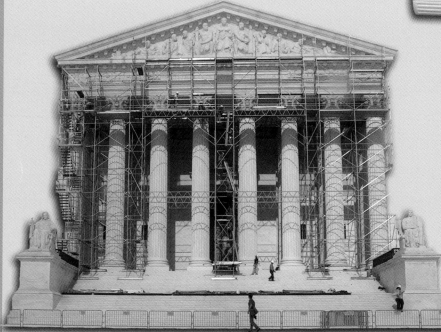

Supreme Court

scaffolding

souvenir
sweatshirt
vendor

street signs

Smithsonian
Institution
Castle

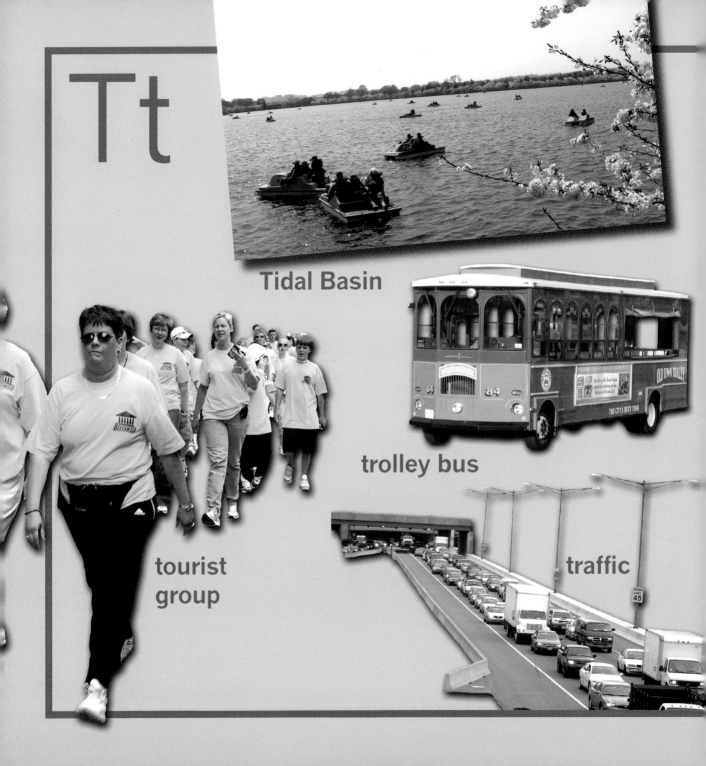

Tt

Tidal Basin

trolley bus

tourist group

traffic

traffic
light

taxis

trash can

Treasury Building

Uu

umbrellas

Union Station

Vv

Viet Nam
Veterans
Memorial

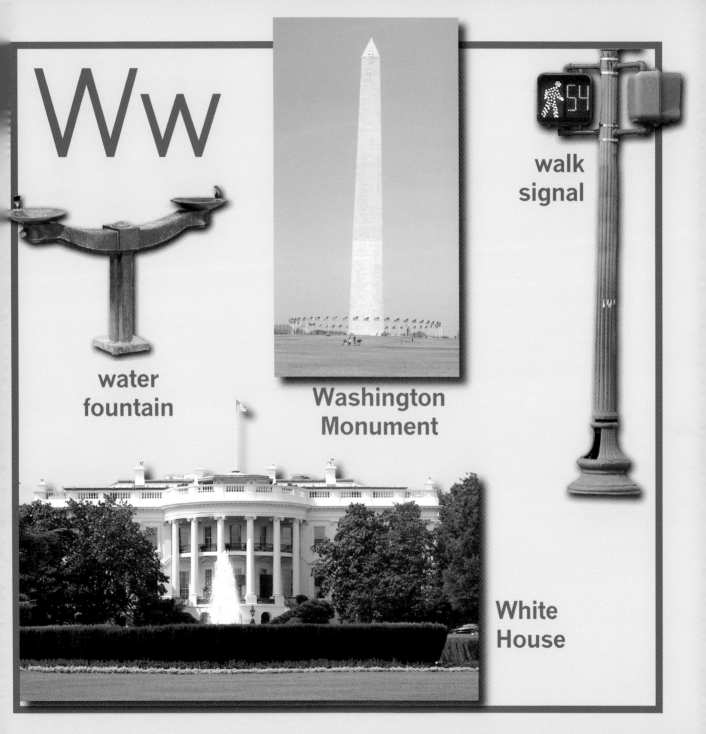

Ww

water
fountain

Washington
Monument

walk
signal

White
House

Xx

Xenia Street

Yy

yellow cab

Zz

zebras
and friends at the
zoo

Murray Hill Books, LLC
P.O. Box 4393
New York, NY 10163

www.murrayhillbooks.com
info@murrayhillbooks.com
SAN 256-3622

Library of Congress Control Number: 2006935624
ISBN 0-9719697-7-9

Photography, Design, and Editing by Robin Segal.
"All 'Bout Cities" is a Registered Trademark.

Look for more "All 'Bout Cities" titles at:

www.allboutcities.com